For Annie and Amelia. K.C.

For Oliver, my brother the greep! N.M.

THE BRAVE LITTLE GRORK
by Kathryn Cave and Nick Maland

Text copyright © Kathryn Cave 2002
Illustrations copyright © Nick Maland 2002

The right of Kathryn Cave to be identified as the
author and Nick Maland as the illustrator of this
work has been asserted by them in accordance with
the Copyright, Designs and Patents Act 1988.

First published by Hodder Children's Books 2002.
This edition published by Friendly Dragon 2015.

www.friendly-dragon.com

A catalogue record for this book is available
from the British Library.

ISBN 978-0-99310-782-5

The Brave Little Grork

written by Kathryn Cave • illustrated by Nick Maland

FRIENDLY DRAGON
BOOKS

This is a **grork**.
Grorks don't like saying hello.
They are shy and easily
frightened.

This is a **greep.**
Greeps love saying hello.
They are not shy. And they almost never get frightened.

The greep and the grork are great friends.
They do most things together.

One day the greep wanted to go to the wood.
He waited and waited while his friend got ready.
It took a long time.

The grork was frightened of getting lost.
He was frightened of wind and rain, and fire and floods.

He was frightened of turples.

He put everything he thought he might need in a bag.
A big bag. Two bags.
'Right,' said the greep. 'Can we go?'
The grork didn't hear him. He was looking for his umbrella.

At the gate, the grork stopped dead.
Something was coming!
'Oh no!' he whispered. 'A turple!'

His heart began to beat very
fast. 'Quick, hide!' he cried,
and dived into the nearest bush.

Only it wasn't a turple.
'Hello, Greep. Where's Grork?'
asked the flurg.

'Hello, Flurg,' said the grork.

The grork scrambled out of the bush.
He felt silly, and he'd ruined his umbrella.
He felt like going home and going to bed.
But he wanted to go to the wood with
the greep, so on he went.

Before long, something flew up out of a field by the road.
The grork's heart began to thump very loud.
'Help! A killer bee!' he cried.
He dived into a ditch to escape.

It wasn't a killer bee. It was a butterfly.

The grork scrambled out of the ditch.
He was covered in mud. Before he
could clean it off, he heard footsteps.
Oh no! He didn't want anyone to see
him looking like that. He took a step
back, and fell into the ditch again.
'Hello, Greep. Hello, Grork,'
said the flurg.

The mud wouldn't clean off.
'Never mind,' said the greep. 'It's just mud. Who cares?'
But the grork did care. He didn't like mud and he hated
being scared of so many things.
'Oh Greep,' he said, 'I wish I was more like you.
I wish I never got scared at all.'

'I get scared too,' said the greep.
'I just think brave thoughts, that's all.'
So the grork practised thinking the
bravest thoughts he could.

This bridge will probably not break, he thought.
He took a deep breath and stepped onto it
as if it was quite safe. And it was!

That mouse is probably not going to bite me,
he thought. He walked past with his knees shaking.
And it scampered into its hole!

The grork was very excited. He'd been brave – twice!
'Thinking brave thoughts works,' he told the greep.
'It really does.'
'It works for me too,' the greep said. 'Usually.'

Suddenly, there they were at the haunted tree.
People said the ghost of an old crow who'd been struck by
lightning swooped down from its branches on stormy nights.

The grork's knees started shaking. Before he could
think brave thoughts, the wind blew and the branches

creee-ee-aked!

'Run!' cried the grork. *'Run for your life!'*

When the grork stopped running
he was deep in the wood.

He didn't know any of the creatures
that lived there. They looked strange
and scary and big. He walked faster
and faster, pretending he knew where
he was. Until he walked smack into
something.

OOF!

It felt like a turple.
It smelled like a turple.
It said 'Ouch!' in a turple's voice.

The grork felt sure that if he opened his eyes he would see it WAS a turple, so he kept them shut. He lay still, holding his breath, hoping the turple would think he was dead.

'Hello Grork. Where's Greep?' said the turple.
All at once the grork knew who it was!
He opened his eyes.

'Oh Flurg, I AM glad to see you,' he said.

They met the greep
at the edge of the wood
and went home singing.

This is the grork.

He is shy and easily frightened
and very brave.
He is frightened of wind and rain,
and fire and floods. He is frightened
of being laughed at, and ghosts.
He is frightened of turples.
Yet he still went to the deep dark
wood and found his way home again.

Hurrah for the brave little grork!